NOW YOU CAN READ....

Cinderella

STORY ADAPTED BY LUCY KINCAID

ILLUSTRATED BY ERIC KINCAID

BRIMAX BOOKS • NEWMARKET • ENGLAND

Cinderella lived in a big house.
She was always busy. Her two
stepsisters made her work hard.
"Cinderella! Sweep the floor!"
"Cinderella! Wash the dishes!"
"Make the beds!"
"Clean the windows!"
Cinderella's work was never done.

Her stepsisters spent half the day
telling Cinderella what to do.
They spent the other half trying
to make themselves pretty.
"Cinderella!
Brush my hair!"
"Cinderella!
Tie my bow!"

"Powder my nose!"
"Fasten my buttons!"

One day a letter arrived at the house.

"There is to be a ball at the palace. We are invited!" shouted the stepsisters.

"Am I invited?" asked Cinderella.

"Even if you are, you cannot go," said her stepsisters. "You will be too busy getting us ready."

The day of the ball came. The
stepsisters kept Cinderella very
busy indeed. There was so much
to do. Poor Cinderella did not
know what to do first.

At last, the stepsisters had gone and the house was quiet. Cinderella sat by the fire and began to cry. "If only I could go to the ball," she wept.

"You SHALL go to the ball," said a voice behind her. Cinderella jumped up in surprise. She thought she was alone in the house.

"Who . . . who are you?" she gasped.

"I am your Fairy Godmother," said the stranger.

"I have come to get you ready for the ball."

"Bring me a pumpkin," said the Fairy Godmother. She turned the pumpkin into a coach.

"Bring me four white mice," said the Fairy Godmother. She turned the mice into four white horses.

"Bring me three lizards," said the Fairy Godmother. They became a coach-driver and two footmen.

"I cannot go to the ball dressed
in rags," said Cinderella sadly.

The Fairy Godmother waved her magic wand once more. Cinderella's rags turned into a beautiful ball-gown. Her bare feet were covered with dainty glass slippers.

"Now you are ready for the ball," said the Fairy Godmother.

"But first, a warning. You must leave before the clock strikes twelve. At twelve everything will change back again."

"I will remember," said Cinderella. "Thank you, dear Fairy Godmother."

Cinderella danced all night with
the Prince. Her stepsisters saw
her, but they did not know it was
Cinderella. They thought she was
a princess.

Cinderella was so
happy she forgot
all about the
Fairy Godmother's
warning. Then
the palace clock
began to strike
the chimes of
midnight. One...
two...three...
"I must go!"
cried Cinderella
and she ran from
the palace.

"Stop! Stop!" cried the Prince. Cinderella did not hear him. As she ran down the palace steps she lost one of her glass slippers. . . . ten . . . eleven . . . TWELVE!!!

The beautiful gown turned into rags. The coach turned into a pumpkin. The mice and the lizards ran away.

The Prince found
her glass slipper
lying on the
palace steps.
He called to
a footman.

"Take this slipper
and find its
owner. I will
marry the girl
it fits."

The footman travelled all over the
kingdom with the slipper. It fitted
no one. At last he came to the
house where Cinderella lived.
"Let me try it!"
said one of the
stepsisters. She
snatched the
slipper from
the footman.
"Look!" she cried.
"A perfect fit."

"No it is not!" shouted the other stepsister. "Your heel is hanging out. Give it to me!" She snatched the glass slipper.

It didn't fit her either, though she tried to pretend that it did. "Is there anyone else in the house who should try the slipper?" asked the footman.

"No!" said both stepsisters together.

"Yes there is," said their father. "Cinderella has not tried it yet."

"The Prince would never marry HER!"
laughed the stepsisters.
"The Prince said everyone must try
the slipper," said the footman.
It fitted Cinderella perfectly.

Her stepsisters were so surprised
they fainted.

The stepsisters still looked
surprised when the Prince and
Cinderella were married.

All these appear in the pages of
the story. Can you find them?

stepsisters

Cinderella

letter

Fairy Godmother